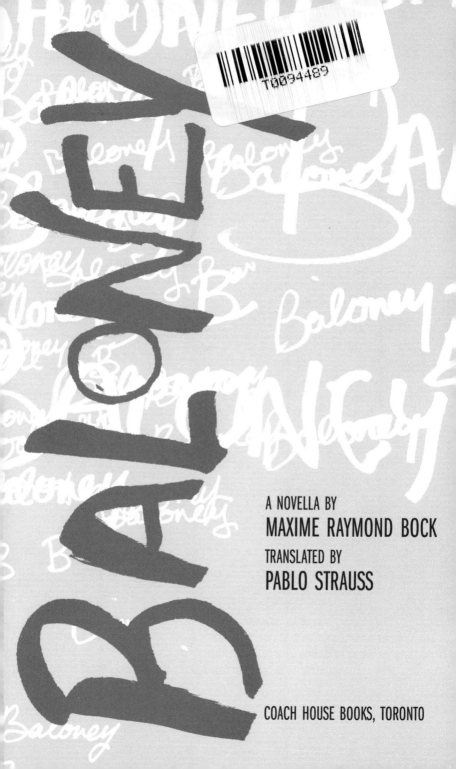

A NOVELLA BY
MAXIME RAYMOND BOCK

TRANSLATED BY
PABLO STRAUSS

COACH HOUSE BOOKS, TORONTO

First English edition. Originally published in French in 2015 as *Des
lames de pierre* by Le Cheval d'Août.

Coach House Books acknowledges the financial support of the Government of Canada through the National Translation Program for Book
Publishing, an initiative of the *Roadmap for Canada's Official Languages
2013-2018: Education, Immigration, Communities,* for our translation activ-
ities. We also thank the Canada Council for the Arts and the Ontario Arts
Council for their generous assistance. We further acknowledge the support
of the Government of Canada through the Canada Book Fund.

LIBRARY AND ARCHIVES CANADA CATALOGUING IN PUBLICATION

Bock, Raymond, 1981-
[Des lames de pierre. English]
    Baloney / by Maxime Raymond Bock ; translated by Pablo Strauss.

Translation of: Des lames de pierre.
ISBN 978-1-55245-339-1 (paperback).

    I. Strauss, Pablo, translator II. Title. III. Title: Des lames de pierre.
English

PS8603.O29D4713 201   C843'.6   C2016-904394-0

Baloney is available as an ebook: ISBN 978 1 77056 468 8 (EPUB), ISBN
978 1 77056 469 5 (PDF), ISBN 978 1 77056 470 1 (MOBI)

Purchase of the print version of this book entitles you to a free digital copy.
To claim your ebook of this title, please email sales@chbooks.com with
proof of purchase or visit chbooks.com/digital. (Coach House Books
reserves the right to terminate the free digital download offer at any time.)

Baloney

1

Like ninety-four other people in the province of Quebec, Robert Lacerte was born on November 18, 1941. It happened in a house on the main street of the small town of Saint-Donat, and later in life, when he saw similarities between his poetry and Gaston Miron's, Robert put it down to their shared homeland in the Laurentians. As if the trees, foxes, river bends, mountains and trails of smoke left behind by vacationers could bring about the genesis of words. But words have a way of finding their own path, and this origin was all he ever had in common with Miron. In the Montreal poetry scene his nickname was 'Baloney.' He never told me why, and I eventually realized he himself didn't know. He was much less ridiculous than the nickname implied, just a tad feeble of body and mind, not entirely equal to the daily struggle of life on the margins, always a touch off the beat, a length behind the others – always, deep down, alone. His weaknesses were clear for all to see, but no one was there when he was flying high. He flailed in silence and died, along with 151 other Québécois, on January 6, 2009, at Maisonneuve-Rosemont Hospital.

Robert remembered so little of his childhood that he managed at times to believe he'd never had one, and he would tell himself, when consciousness returned after a fit of severe pain, that life isn't a continuous flow of which we retain only fragments but an arrangement of broken, unconnected tableaux, accidents separated by cracks where everything is erased. Digging into his past, he might remember an event, a day, sometimes even an entire season, but then there was emptiness, until the next memory, when people re-emerged older and places had changed shape and colour after disintegrating into darkness. He once told me that was why he wrote, to prolong the time he existed, to have fewer of these moments of nothingness. But another time he told me that none of it mattered – memory, words, photos, film – because by their very nature the chasms everything disappears into may well be unfathomable, infinitely deeper than any traces we try to leave, and that's why we're no better off than the dead.

For Robert, life didn't begin when two gametes fused to create a zygote, or when a hairy head emerged from his screaming mother, but on the evening of his first memory when, from his crib tucked under a staircase, he first felt fear of something lurking in the back of the dim room where his brothers lay snoring like two-stroke engines. He then experienced a diffuse series of events as he sat on the parlour floor in piss-stained cotton diapers or at the table, banging his plate with a spoon until one of his sisters yanked it from him with threats. Then others, in clearer focus – games of hide-and-seek out in the fields, fights lost to brothers too strong for him, running bare-headed through the rain, hunting stray cats for the mayor's public-health campaign. Robert's childhood wasn't a difficult one. Nor was it easy. Village life in a French-Canadian backwater in the mid-twentieth century was tough. There was squalor of every stripe: dignified poverty, deep-black misery, filthy indigence, half-bred want, laugh-despite-it-all scarcity, pious simplicity, revolting privation, resigned paucity, mortal destitution and countless others. The Lacertes' poverty fell on the comfortable end of the spectrum. Saint-Donat had electricity and Old Man Lacerte had ably managed his general store. When his three eldest sons took over, they turned it into a hardware store that supported their parents, who still pitched in when they could, and the siblings who were still too young to work.

Robert was the second-last child of his generation. Before him had passed forty brothers, sisters and cousins; after came but one baby sister who alone enjoyed the usual privileges of the last-born child. The older ones already had families of their own and weren't much for travel, so Robert scarcely saw them. He stayed home with his aging parents. On the rare occasions when the whole family gathered, the other children called him Fake Uncle or Old Wart or Fuddy-Duddy.

Who knows what goes on in the mind of a child whose formative years are spent among the elderly. His course was charted, he just had to slide into the groove and move forward. There was the dirt path to the schoolhouse, worn into the grass along the stand of trees between two fields. The muddy road they all trod single file to church. And to escape, the path to the thicket where everyone snuck off at some point to make out and feel up their first crushes. Robert's was the daughter of a family of tourists who'd come down from Montreal to ski Mount Jasper, a girl with extraordinary blue eyes, teeth so incredibly large they prevented her mouth from closing, and a body inaccessible beneath her winter coat. The kiss was far from pleasing, and years would pass before he tried another. Of all his relatives, Robert was close to one only, his brother Yves, his elder by one year and seven days. The two boys' birthdays were marked by a single celebration halfway through the week between them.

The first event of note in Robert's life occurred when he was fourteen. He took a trip to what may as well have been the end of the known world, five and a half hours by train and horse-drawn sled northwest of Saint-Donat, to spend a winter, the only one he ever would, in a lumber camp. With its outhouses and stables, kitchen and bunkhouses and large dining hall, the sprawling log cabin was at once modern and archaic. Heat came from wood stoves but the lights were electric, powered by a turbine spinning in a stream a hundred paces off, or a gas generator when the river froze in winter. There was an electric range, a giant cast-iron woodstove and a shortwave radio transmitter and receiver from the First World War. Robert was too spindly to chop trees or mill boards, too weak to drive horses. For a kid like him, the camp's hierarchy was clear: it would be at least ten years before he touched the brand-new gas-powered light-weight chainsaws and American skidders that Canadian International Paper was bringing in. But Robert had no desire to be a logger, loved his fingers too much to risk losing them to frostbite or a falling axe. He didn't want to be anything in particular. He had reached the end of compulsory schooling without enough faith in the saints to try for the novitiate, or in himself to consider the classical curriculum. Denis Berval, a boy one year older than Robert, worked alongside him keeping the camp running and the books in order. They cooked for the thirty ogres who stumbled back to camp at dusk, frozen and starving, and did it all over again at dawn so the men could set out into the bush with full stomachs. They cleaned the dormitory and the stables and ordered food and fuel, tools and clothing. Ayotte, who'd drawn the short straw at the start of the contract, picked up supplies and mail at a cache every two months. A forced complicity arose between Denis and Robert. Neither made friends easily, and neither was a natural cook or housekeeper. They didn't know how to run a kitchen, had never shovelled manure. But their shared workload and the cold forced them together, and when they finally had some free time between mopping the floors and cooking up huge pots of soup with peameal bacon, they would sit and play some cards or dice, sweating next to the stoves, swearing they had nothing in common with their brothers or fathers or the men they slaved away for in this godforsaken outpost. They were both right, in their way.

Denis, the son of the Saint-Hippolyte notary, showed up to camp in his Sunday best. He may have been only one year older, but his education was beyond anything Robert aspired to. That a mind like his should be sent to wash pots at lumber camp suggested punishment, but Robert couldn't bring himself to ask Denis what the hell he was doing there. Everyone understood the local politics behind Robert's presence: part of the camp's supply order went through the Saint-Donat hardware store. Robert was a favour the Lacertes did the Company, an extra pair of hands paid only in morning porridge, evening soup and plentiful heat. Robert never found out what Denis earned for his work. They figured out a way to work together cheerfully, bemoaning their fate only when the loggers were at work, and even then they always found something to laugh about: the long curly red hairs that worked their way into the building's every nook and cranny, the dead-rat smell in a bag left under a bunk, the shit-stained long johns frozen stiff behind the backhouse, the socks with holes so big you wouldn't know which end to put your foot in. They were on their own until evening, except once every two weeks when one of the loggers stayed at camp and split a cord of wood to heat the kitchen. Those days passed in silence. The boys did the dishes and cleaned to the sound of splitting logs. On other days, they chatted about their sisters and mothers, the girls they had seen, impossible things, the cast of the light, the splinters in their fingers, the dishes to be washed, the porridge, the liberal professions, horse piss, village stores. Denis had the mysterious gift of perceiving the hidden faces of objects, people, actions and ideas. He always used words Robert knew, yet it seemed that, by naming the world in this way, Denis conjured up another reality, a field of energy drawn tightly around what each term evoked, and thus the frame surrounding things, creatures and concepts was knit together of some unknown fabric. Through his new friend, Robert had access to an exclusive space whose existence he would never have otherwise suspected, a world that closed up behind Denis's words like the wake behind a boat.

Times were changing. The company was adopting modern ways and equipment. The lumberjacks talked about a union, but in their hearts still cleaved to the old ways, loved yelling at workhorses harnessed to stumps and the feel of the axe thrumming in their hands. Above all, they had grown used to the rule of the cook who'd been with them eight winters, a heavy-set man with a huge nose bulbous from rosacea whose qualities included never getting hairs in the porridge (he didn't have any) and putting any man in line with a single look. They said that he'd died over the summer. They said that he'd gone off to cook somewhere else in the Pays d'en Haut, that he'd had enough of the smell of gas oil and pine and given up camp life to be a stevedore, that he'd killed three whores in Mont-Laurier, that he'd been given the boot by the Company and the less they knew about it the better. The two new hands slept one above the other in the bunks closest to the kitchen so they could start the morning porridge without bothering the men and go to sleep as quietly as possible once the dishes were done and everyone was in bed. Most of the time the frozen loggers found the soup too cold. They called the cooks little faggots or skunk-fuckers, and the boys could hear angry shouts from the far end of the bunkhouse ordering them to stop making the mattresses creak and get their hands out of their pants. One night when it seemed the insults might turn to blows, Robert and Denis stacked the sacks of grain along the kitchen wall, protected by a row of mousetraps, hung the sides of salt beef from the rafters, and pushed the bunkbed into the empty pantry. They just barely managed to squeeze it in, and they couldn't shut the door behind themselves, but at least that way they got some peace and quiet. The lumberjacks could go right on insulting them in the bunkhouse, raise a ruckus, sing all the songs they wanted – the kids felt safe. Robert took the top bunk. There was so little space between the mattress and the ceiling that if he wasn't careful turning onto his side, he tore holes in the shoulders of his woollens. They froze in their little alcove, but cold was a fundamental element of the camp, like air or water. It didn't enter anyone's mind to complain. And they were lucky to be closer to the stovepipes than the other men. Robert often climbed into his cubby when he had an hour of downtime, to finally sleep without the sound of thirty men snoring.

One mid-January afternoon, a jingling bell and a *Whoa!* from the driver turned the boys from their cleaning. Denis cried out, unusually happy to see the winter's second delivery. The first, in November, had arrived in the middle of the night and a week late. It wasn't a fond memory. Ayotte, covered with half an inch of frost and in the throes of vertigo, had jumped at the boys, seeing two evil spirits with putrefying faces. The lumberjacks had to step in and knock him out. This time the horses had made a good trip of it, the day was cold and clear, and Ayotte was cracking jokes about the previous delivery. While he warmed up at the stove, Robert and Denis unloaded the bundle of mail, last month's newspapers, two jerry cans of fuel, a side of beef, a new oven element, two metal files, six axe heads, hundred-pound sacks of oats and buckwheat and big bags of laundry. Though the sled appeared empty, Denis went out one final time and came back holding a packet the size of a music box, wrapped in brown paper and tied up with string, which he immediately slid under his bed. When the lumberjacks went back out to swing their axes, Denis pulled out the package and called Robert over. He severed the string with his teeth and tore off the brown paper. Fifteen books, a hundred-odd sheets of paper and a few pencils spilled out onto the floor and mattress.

That was the end of their afternoon naps. Denis became distracted and less thorough with his work. He read a quick line every time he passed by the bed, took more frequent trips to the outhouse and burned an oil lamp in the alcove to read by once the dishes were done. It fell on Robert to make up the work that Denis left unfinished. With no partner for cards or dice in a camp that felt suddenly empty, Robert couldn't help taking an interest in the written word. Fifteen books and nothing but French-Canadian verse. Robert was wholly ignorant of poetry, though he'd managed to sound out the opening of Routhier's 'Ô Canada.' The first lines of the first volume he opened, by Alain Grandbois, seemed at once obvious and empty, a series of words dumped out one after another. There was nothing to understand. Perfect: he hadn't understood a thing. The next day he tried again with Gilles Hénault. Even worse. He went back to the kitchen. A few days later Denis started writing little chunks of text, leaving large white spaces on the paper – not frugal practice in such an isolated camp, Robert couldn't help pointing out. By way of answer, Denis opened Anne Hébert's *Les songes en équilibre* on his bed and invited Robert to take in and compare the positive and negative capability of the black and the white spaces. The pile of blank sheets began to dwindle and Robert wondered whether he shouldn't take a few before they were gone. Denis gave him four. Robert slid them under his mattress.

A new rhythm began to take hold, a break from the routine. The days grew longer but the cold dug in its heels. Robert cultivated an interest in Crémazie, Fréchette and Gill, who were much richer in evocative power, to his mind, due to the smaller spaces they left on the page. Denis recited verse while scrubbing pots and deboning hunks of meat. The lumberjacks went about their business. In the evenings they would emerge from the bush in clouds of steam to slurp down their soup and stink up the bunkhouse with their pipes and roll-your-owns. They were getting rougher with the boys. The stables weren't clean enough: luckily, the shit froze the second it hit the ground, but sometimes the loggers had to shovel it themselves. The soup was disgusting, the porridge too sticky, the beans too mushy. Robert and Denis counted the days till spring.

Big Lambert came in from the bush at noon one day in March, treading silently over a foot of powder so fluffy that, once disturbed by his feet, it took flight again. As he approached the pile of logs to split behind the kitchen, he peered through the window and saw the two boys bent over books in front of the furnace, a plaid blanket spread over their laps. That night, standing on an overturned washbasin in the bunkhouse, he entertained the men whose cheeks were flushed with brandy and throats raw from smoke. Their raucous laughter as he slowly, loudly read from one of Denis's books, following along with his finger, concealed a crude, contagious fury. The recital dragged on at least ten pages, and the boys heard every word, never taking their eyes from the little lumps of crud in their dishwater, even when two lumberjacks poked their heads into the kitchen archway to say, 'Looks like we got some fiery virgins here, boys,' and

'Hey, it's Mardi Gras, come do a little show for us.' The young poets tried to decline but felt themselves shoved from behind into the centre of the circle. Over the muttering and clinking of flasks, Denis was forced to read a few pages of Saint-Denys Garneau. He was so parched that each syllable stuck to the roof of his mouth. He felt outside himself as he turned the trembling pages, standing a few inches taller than Robert, much skinnier than other boys his age. His patchy blond moustache was darkened with sweat. Robert felt sorry for him. He also felt violently naked. The book held over his pelvis like a fig leaf afforded no protection. After a mocking ovation, the men demanded more. They were drunk. Insults flew. The pleasure of humiliating wanted only a spark of weakness to flare up. Robert leafed frantically through his William Chapman, tearing out half pages, cracking the leather binding, then pausing a second and breathing deeply before he launched into a passage:

> The breakup of the wide Etchemin, that swims
> its imprisoned waves under the ice,
> And, with a cant hook in hand, proud and strong
> floaters drag the heavy logs, stranded on shore
> Or on the ice clad, jagged rocks, whole forests
> That ran aground, are slid across the freshets
> By the valiant woodcutters of Dorchester and their iron
> Toward the giant river that carries them to the sea.
> It's been days with no peace nor relief,
> The bold log rollers singing while they work.

Turn after turn, on the riverbanks and in their long canoes,
They work on – with all the drive of heroes –
Commanded by a leader with the shoulders of Hercules.

Their job is mighty hard but no one backs down
– The Company name takes the place of a flag –
When they must risk their shirt or their skin …

In a trance, Robert failed to notice the astonishment of the men, who now sat rapt, or the brief silence that descended every time he turned a page. Ayotte put a hand on his shoulder. Robert kept on reading, his cracking voice a grotesque yodel. Ayotte shook him gently. 'Stop. Go finish the dishes. And make sure the porridge is on time tomorrow. We've got to finish cutting the trail along Lac Vert. Before the melt. Understand what that means, son?' The men went back to their bunks; the boys walked shakily to their quarters. From that night on, the porridge and soup were to the lumberjacks' liking and the stables were swept and the dishes gleamed. A week later, when the time came for a final run to the cache, Denis, with a notary's son's promise of reward, convinced Ayotte to take the boys along. Denis left everything he owned behind. Robert brought his four sheets of paper, folded in his pocket and covered in writing on all eight sides.

2

I think about Robert a lot. I can hear his voice, smell his rank cigarette-and-coffee breath and the greasy stench of his apartment, and feel his frail handshakes and the lightness against my chest during our quick hugs when we greeted and said goodbye. We met a year and a half before he died. It's not much in a lifetime, just long enough for a damaged creature to quickly complete the business of wasting away. Sometimes, toward the end, what he said had only the slightest purchase on our world and seemed poised to fade to silence after the next comma. He would forget that he had already told me certain stories, and on their second or third tellings they would veer off in different directions, but deep down I knew he spoke truthfully each and every time, more truthfully than me, more truthfully than anyone. He was the one who made me see the vanity of my own life.

When I picture him now – his emaciated body and translucent skin, his matted beard and sticky hair, forever wearing the same worn-out jeans and T-shirts, eternally hunched over his coffee table, rolling the cigarettes that ate away at his lungs and caused him to spit up bloody gobs of phlegm, like full stops after the coughing fits that interrupted our discussions every ten minutes – the present comes into focus for me as a single whole, my senses open up and take it all in with no filter, and I concentrate in order to ward off my uneasiness with the idea that as soon as each moment unfolds it's gone, we can't take any of it with us, except a faint outline that can only be filled in through imagination. I walk in the park next to my house and on the sidewalk next to the Rivière des Prairies, where families enjoy the still-warm afternoons, though October is upon us. I have fun with my kids, climbing monkey bars and chasing each other around the playground. I strive to be mindful of it all, to push my consciousness to its limit, to soak it all up. It brings me a degree of well-being, makes me feel like part of an indefinable skein of meaning, a great force intelligible only through spirituality, a holistic intuition that draws me in but that I will have no choice but to let go of once I realize that, of everything that has just happened, only spectral traces remain.

At that point, with two manuscripts rejected and a third accepted, subject to an impossible rewrite, by a friend who ran a small press, I had turned my back on poetry. But not on poets. I still went to launches and readings, and sometimes parties – since finishing university and having children, these were my only chances to see this circle of acquaintances, where I still had a few friends. I was now a minor player. I no longer stepped up to the mic to read. A new crop of good-looking young poets with a strong sense of showmanship had arrived on the scene and pushed me to the margins. The esteem certain people had once held me in was rekindled for a while when I published a short collection of wide-ranging stories of uneven quality. It garnered a brief review in one of the papers and a few blog posts. Two or three people told me they'd read and enjoyed it.

I was looking for a way to start writing again and coming up blank. The same words saturated my mind, but their meanings seemed to have evaporated. I could no longer read anything beyond what crossed my desk for copy-editing – poorly conceived advertising, business reports written in gibberish, tourism and mechanics magazines, literary manuscripts scarcely better than my own. My kids were taking over my entire life, sucking me dry to the very marrow; it felt like I was withering away for them while they flourished. Bags were appearing under my eyes, and not even a good night's sleep, when I actually got one, could make them go away. I lived in terror of my pen. When I sensed the approach of a moment I might be able to spend writing, on weekends when the kids were at their grandparents' or during nervous nights when I couldn't take another second of listening to Joannie sleep, I would squander them fucking around on the internet. When Robert came into my life, one June evening in Parc Hochelaga, where the Poetry Van was making its rounds, I had more or less resigned myself to the idea that I would never write another word.

The poets were taking turns at the mic in front of the van, reading from crumpled-up bits of paper, books and magazines. I was spending my evening chasing Chloé, my youngest, through the crowd. In between two performances, while I chatted with an acquaintance, she got away from me again and I found her sitting on a park bench beside an old man. He was looking at her, smiling, a smoke dangling from the corner of his mouth. As I grabbed my daughter I said hi to the old man and thanked him, then promptly forgot all about it. A month later, I recognized him when the Poetry Van stopped in Centre-Sud. He wasn't just a park regular drawn by a pop-up artistic performance – he'd been following the Poetry Van around town, a constant presence on the outskirts of the crowd, sitting on a bench, just close enough to hear the amplified voices. He didn't react to the readings, seemed content to sit there smoking and listening. I approached him and he nodded, and asked me why I hadn't brought my daughter this time. I joked that the family unit could be a prison cell, and I was out on furlough. He showed me a piece of paper folded up in his tobacco pouch, said he was trying to decide whether to read at the open mic at the end of the event. He didn't get the chance. Darkness was descending. We went out for a few pints.

3

Nothing much happened in the six hours it took Robert and Denis to flee camp. Their apprehension and excitement had time to settle in the sleigh, where the boys huddled together under the raw wool blanket, pitching and rolling and being bumped into the air by what lay beneath the snow. The next leg was spent face-to-face watching winter roll by through the train window. From Denis's initial yelp of joy as camp receded from view to Robert's mumbled goodbye when he got off at Saint-Jérôme, not one word was uttered, not even by Ayotte, who'd given tacit notice the moment he agreed to drive the young kids home, leaving the lumberjacks to their own devices for the rest of the contract. Ayotte commanded his horses with an array of onomatopoeias. After a half-hour break behind a stand of firs to warm by a fire and cook three cans of beans in tomato sauce, he dropped the boys off by a red-and-yellow sign sticking out of the snow a few yards from a locked shed next to the train track. Ayotte and his sleigh disappeared into the sugar bush.

In Saint-Jérôme, Robert also headed off into the woods, on a sleigh or perhaps a truck. He resurfaced two years later standing next to his brother Yves at the family home. They were mourning their mother, whose heart had given out at fifty-four. Her widow, Robert's father, sat in the centre of the gathering. The extended family had come together for a final look at a body distended by eighteen pregnancies. It was hard to recognize her under all the makeup. An aunt kicked up a fuss because there was no prie-dieu in front of the coffin, and Robert slipped off with only the cloth bag he had slung over his shoulder, not dressed for the fall weather. He walked to the end of Saint-Donat's main street, boots lifting the leaves off the ground, and turned up in Sherbrooke in 1961.

The hot water went cold after three minutes, the ceiling plaster either crumbled into a fine grey dust that gathered on the floor or broke off in chunks as big as your hand, and you had to wear multiple layers through winter, but it was here, in the apartment on Rue de l'Assomption, that Robert felt at home and in control of his environment for the first time. It was here in his bachelor suite that he got acquainted with what young men must learn: regular drunkenness, occasional orgasms, hunger allayed with salt and fat, and that unyielding, all-encompassing loneliness that plays tricks with your senses until you can hear your heart beating even while you smash glasses against the wall. In Sherbrooke and its outskirts, Robert spent years working for a succession of bosses who took no notice of him. On an assembly line he snipped the rubber filaments off car-door seals. At a hardware store, as gruffly as possible, he sold tools and lumber to burly men like the ones he'd fled the lumber camp to escape. In a bakery he came in at dawn to bake bread for harried housekeepers. There were construction sites and warehouses. He worked in fresh forest air and he inhaled paint fumes and he laboured on bridges and on roads. Only once safely home in his bachelor apartment could Robert finally return to himself. And there, on a little bookshelf salvaged from the sidewalk and forced into plumb with metal brackets, he began to assemble the volumes of French-Canadian poetry discussed in Camille Roy's *Manuel d'histoire de la littérature canadienne de langue française*. With bird feathers he collected on the banks of the Magog River and sharpened to a bevel, he copied excerpts out into his notebooks, drumming on the table to count syllables. Twice a year he phoned Yves, who had little to say about life as an accountant in their hometown.

At twenty-four, Robert got a job cooking at Bradley's on King Street, a poorly ventilated family restaurant where pearls of fat collected on his forehead. The pass-through afforded a view of students in large glasses and gorgeous young women who spoke loudly and moved gracefully, radiating confidence and intelligence. He couldn't let his hair grow the way other young men were starting to – Bradley wouldn't allow it – but he could listen to the same music and read the same books, whose titles sometimes reached him over the clamour of the kitchen. He would return to his apartment with the memories of these women, their exposed shoulders and beehives and kohl-darkened eyelids, and masturbate before going to sleep and upon waking up to what he imagined lay under their dresses.

The job improved when Robert started going out with one of the waitresses. She was as reserved as he was, but somehow developed a crush on him. After a few days of ignoring each other, they started saying hello, then exchanging smiles, and then, more easily than Robert could have ever imagined, spending time together after work, and finally sharing a bed. Nicole had grown up playing in overgrown empty lots and muddy front yards, exploring the banks of the Saint-François River, which had taken the life of one of her sisters. Now she lived in a rented attic room in an old building on Rue du Conseil. It was tight for two but fit them to a tee. After sex Robert would turn to face the wall, pressed between Nicole's body on one side and the angled attic wall on the other, breathing in the current of fresh air rising up beside the mattress. Nicole was three years older than him. Men had caused her problems she preferred not to discuss, but she wasn't going to live her life like an old maid in her attic room. She had plenty of friends and hung out at the fringes of a circle of students and artists. Robert had won her over with his gentleness and docility more than his charms, but also with the mystery of his writings. He kept them to himself the whole time they were together, save a single ongoing series of poems he thought were passionate. These declined in frequency and intensity after the first year, then slowed to a trickle of a few insipid verses every four months. Robert wanted love but couldn't understand what it would do to him. He tried to force it by sucking in his diaphragm and abs to make something in his chest contract and maybe secrete a new fluid, release some kind of magic. He'd been reading love poetry long enough to know how love was represented, was all too familiar with telluric currents and enflamed physical sensations, trees and animals, sugary odours, uncontrollable enthusiasms. That, at any rate, was how he put it in his writings. Seeking out new forms of expression to convey this state, he turned to the poets. Roland Giguère, Jean-Guy Pilon: nothing clicked. At least his needs were met. Nicole and Robert hung around with Sherbrooke's other young people, went to a Nana Mouskouri concert, watched a water-skiing competition on Lac des Nations, saw plays and bad *yé-yé* shows and student cabarets at the Faculty of Arts. They'd go hiking in the woods, boldly drink wine straight from the bottle, smoke the odd joint. Most nights were now spent together at one of their apartments, but when Nicole suggested moving into his place, to save money, Robert demurred. He wanted to keep their feelings pure by avoiding the pitfalls of routine.

The grains of sand settled. Nicole broke her wrist falling on the King Street sidewalk and lived off her savings until they were gone. Robert made a deal with Bradley: to keep Nicole's job he'd give up weekend days off until she got better. The next summer, in his building's laundry room, he discovered the body of a man who had hanged himself with his belt. He'd pushed off, the belt had broken, and now his body lay behind the washing machines, legs spread, one arm behind his back and another over his head, like a diver in twist position. His face was grey, his thick tongue was hanging out, his pants were stained with urine. Robert felt bad for repeatedly putting off doing laundry that day – maybe if he'd gone down earlier he might have caught the suicidal man before he climbed the ladder up to the heating pipe sticking out of the ceiling; they could have talked, shared a laugh about the new second-floor tenant with the shapely ass, or the last Sinners concert. It might have been enough to save the man's life. Robert got over his guilt in a few weeks, and the event inspired a series of poems on the battle between chance and destiny.

They went to bars where Nicole's friends talked about fashion, politics and rock and roll, and private parties where they dropped acid together for the first time. That week Robert burned one hamburger patty too many, and Bradley fired him in front of the whole staff. Nicole, eyes cast down, went on serving fries. Robert went back to his job baking for the housekeepers. His new schedule was at odds with Nicole's. He'd get home in the early afternoon and use his free time to write and sleep, alone in the apartment. Come evening, he'd head to the restaurant, take a seat at the counter near the pass-through and watch his former co-workers as he waited for Nicole's shift to end. Then it was up to her attic to drink and smoke, fight and make up. They talked about getting married. She'd wear a blue dress, he'd sport massive sideburns, they'd honeymoon at Niagara Falls and then have kids. Sober sex was getting lacklustre. Robert was ashamed that he seemed to be coming earlier and earlier, whereas in the early days he'd proven more than once that he could last as long as he wanted. Nicole kept telling him not to turn their lovemaking into a competition, and he agreed, but then one night he shot his load before even entering her. After that, intoxicated sex was the only kind they had.

One Saturday at the bar with Nicole's friends, she and Robert sat next to another couple they'd seen around but never plucked up the courage to introduce themselves to. Jeannette and Simon were so good-looking it hurt. Jeannette held her long, slim cigarettes between two slender white-and-red fingers as she glanced sideways with eyes outlined in black, smiling and nodding slightly at every comment made by Simon, who conducted the table with hand movements and conversation on one of the many subjects he knew better than anyone else. Nicole rarely had much to add, and Robert just listened. When he did make a joke, everyone laughed, but not for the same reasons. Jeannette and Nicole got up to go dance, and long after they stopped, they stayed standing by the bar, deep in conversation, glasses held daintily aloft, breaking into laughter and leaning in to make themselves heard by speaking right into each other's ears, and grabbing other friends as they passed by, spinning free and easy under coloured spotlights. At one point they came back to get their coats from the table and then went outside, arm in arm, and only returned half an hour later, clothes smelling of fall, breath pungent with weed.

Simon and Robert spent the whole evening at the table. Simon could confidently expound a theory on even the most trivial question, but was glib when it came to serious matters. While the men were alone, he gave Robert space to open up, and his friend told him about the loneliness of Saint-Donat, the time he fractured his ulna and the legendary snowstorm at lumber camp, when it blew so hard in the clearing at the edge of the woods that the snowflakes climbed *up* to the sky. Simon was a painter. His father was a doctor and art lover – at one time an intimate of local scribe Alfred DesRochers – and he left Simon free to pursue a bohemian existence, all expenses paid. Simon and Jeannette lived together in a massive apartment in the Old North Ward, with so much natural light even the wood on every surface did nothing to darken the rooms. Robert realized he and Nicole had been there before, on a serious bender of which he remembered only the dizziness induced by the booze and the crowd, and the paintings hanging from every wall and leaning in stacks on the floor. Simon thought it was hilarious that they'd spent an evening together without noticing, and started reliving the night in minute detail, making fun of the 'regionalist frame of mind' of the *Prisme d'yeux* manifesto and dissecting why it was unfortunate that he and all his friends played into the hands of the Man by partying so hard all week while they were being robbed blind at every turn. He told stories of his family vacationing with people who had signed *Refus global*. Then he pulled a notebook from his satchel to read Robert his poems. The pages were filled with sketches with a flawless sense of line – there was no evidence of reworking – and the verse was inscribed with the same elegant fountain pen. The calligraphy was a work of art in its own right. Every ascender and descender, downstroke and branching stroke, crossbar and dot, stretched into flourishes that glided around the letters like birds, then sidled up to the figures in every drawing. Robert was impressed by what he could hear as Simon read over the loud rock music. He only took out his own notebook later, after Simon expressed his admiration for fixed verse forms, which required a special mastery of the various but invariably invasive rules of prosody. To navigate such a labyrinth one had to know how to count as well as write. No sooner had Robert opened his notebook than Simon was off on an extempore tangent about the visual composition of the eight blocks of text that comprised the two sonnets. Robert was too shy to read his poems to his new friend. When the girls got back to the table, the discussion stagnated. A third of a pitcher languished on the table. All four agreed it would be nice to do it again sometime, and they walked awhile together, making as much noise and steam as they could, until each couple took a side at the intersection, shouting farewell remarks into the cold air until they could no longer make out the words.

Robert rose before the sun to go get covered with flour at the bakery, where he thought of Nicole's and Jeannette's asses as he kneaded dough. After work he'd go home to wash and sleep, then wake up in the middle of the afternoon and check the progress of the cracks in the ceiling, noting that he was once again covered in white powder, just a different one. The painting Simon had given him took up half a wall and was worth five dollars more each day, in Robert's estimation, because of the new details he saw and could swear hadn't been there the previous night. Nicole was getting prettier and prettier, though nothing had changed in her clothes or makeup, while he grew fatter and one of his incisors turned black. It was a baker's cavity, not the smoking, as he claimed. The four friends drank down whole barrels and smoked up entire fields. The guys did mescaline and dreamed Mexican dreams. Bartenders waved when they walked in, on time for the start of their shift. Even an infestation of ladybugs in Nicole's room was a source of joy: Robert was thrilled they ate the spiders he often saw around the apartment. Even when he couldn't see them, he could feel an invisible tickling.

The two couples frequented poetry readings, and one night shared a bench with the poet Gaston Gouin, who Simon knew through friends of friends. The encounter whetted Robert's poetic desire, and an ecstatically productive period ensued. He borrowed a volume of Prévert and changed the size of the writing pads he was burning through no fewer than six times. The piles of loose pages above his bookshelf climbed higher.

There was no inter-couple swapping. They were all very free in theory, and Simon and Jeannette had tried group sex once before meeting Robert and Nicole, but everyone could see that the risk was too great with their friendship at stake. It was more than just friendship, though: Robert was starting to feel the thing he'd waited for so long, that promise countless words in books had never quite delivered. It was just like in the stories and poems, something blooming in his heart, right next to the ball of anguish, inspired by Jeannette's jawline and the contours of her hips in tights and the perfection of her clothed breasts (he'd never seen them naked), the tone they all used to say hello and goodbye when they saw each other for the first time in three days, how Simon looked him square in the eyes, like an arrow piercing a straw target, and talked like a young man content to know it all, managing to maintain his balance, bare feet on a tightrope, no matter how wasted he got; that stupid laugh they all passed around so effortlessly.

Nicole served fries, Robert baked bread, Jeannette made a name for herself on local stages, Simon hung out in the woods and painted in his studio on cloudless days. His first one-man show, at the gallery of the university cultural centre, was a modest success whose proceeds were swiftly reinvested in new canvases and a brick of hash. A ritual took hold: afternoon would find them in the Old North Ward, drunk by three in the afternoon, stacks of cigarettes smoked, the guys writing and reading their poems aloud at their table or standing up in the corner of some barroom. Simon would brandish a wooden-spoon microphone and shake his hips at the end of each stanza. Then they'd pick up Nicole and head for the bar or the theatre, where Jeannette would meet them later, costumed as a marquise, sylph or housewife. When there was a fire on the ground floor of her building, Nicole moved into Jeannette and Simon's place. Robert followed, using his bachelor pad only for after-work naps, writing and nocturnal meetings with a new group of friends Simon invited when the girls went out without them.

Everyone in this new circle had legitimate grounds for being pissed off. The newspaperman, bilious over his paper's coverage of the Domtar strike, turned his back on *La Tribune* and spent his life running down every lead in the labour conflict. The guy who'd worked with Robert at the rubber factory had lost half his left index finger, lengthwise, then been threatened with a broken leg by his own union reps. The former priest had turned in his collar in his mid-thirties and was making up for lost time by undressing as many women as he could. A rotating cast of students would show up wasted and leave long before the next meeting date had been set. All were poets, in their way. The meetings felt more like hate groups than reading circles, except when Gaston Gouin was there, like a ray of light in the mire. What they discussed in these meetings was so frustrating and deeply demoralizing that their anger readily jumped a notch to fury, and punches were exchanged.

The group wanted to step up and take action, but they couldn't decide between vandalizing the Department of Business Administration at Sherbrooke's English-language university and a nighttime fire at the rubber factory owned by a British–Canadian conglomerate. Robert voted for the factory he hated. They could casually walk in with the rest of the workers at the start of the morning shift, hide behind the massive pipes at the bottom of the southern stairwell and then set to work once the moon rose. Robert's truculence was starting to bleed into his dealings with the world outside the group. He would be livid if Nicole showed up late for a date, was convinced a bakery colleague was an RCMP plant, was suddenly critical of Jeannette whose beauty, he claimed, brought all kinds of riff-raff to the parties at their massive apartment. He got in a fight with a man who butted in line at the grocery store, chewed out an old lady who asked for his seat on the bus, stopped washing his hands after pissing at the bakery. One night in the Old North they dropped acid, and in the shimmer of a strobe light he saw angular animals and hemlock needles coming out of the woodwork, gathering in the shadows of branches undulating on the wall of the double living room, transfigured as henchmen, and clicking insects leaping toward his face in response to orders issued through the loudspeakers. Robert fled through the back door and reappeared two days later. The next day at dawn the head baker, with a boot blocking the door, told Robert he'd had quite enough of his unannounced absences. Robert surprised himself when he reacted by throwing up on the window. At least his rent was paid.

Simon showed up one day around noon, while Robert was still napping. He was literally hopping on his feet, had no discernible irises and had purchased a four-door Valiant.

It was time to head south. Jeannette had been accepted at the Montreal Conservatory, she was leaving in three days, they'd get back together after the trip, he needed company. A few weeks, a couple months, max. They could carry out their action when they got back; the Revolution would wait. Robert put on a pair of black sunglasses and slid his plan of attack for the factory under the defrocked priest's door.

Nicole was lying on the kitchen table in a state of disbelief. All her friends were disappearing. Did her lover not love her anymore? She didn't want to go back to living alone in the attic room with the spiders. Robert made promises: they'd be back soon, she'd easily find a waitressing job in Montreal, she'd just have to move in with Jeannette, and as for love, well, despite what was happening this morning, she would always be 'the most beautiful of petals kissed by the sublimated dew.' The guys got in the Valiant and stopped at the post office, where Robert sent his brother Yves a key, a cheque signed by Simon and the assignment to come to Sherbrooke and empty his apartment of furniture and writings by the end of the month. Then they drove south. Each had a bag of clothes and a few virgin notebooks on the back seat. A motorbike was heading toward them, followed closely by a black car. Simon recognized Gaston Gouin and reached out his window to wave. The bike shot past into space/time, like a missile. He said he didn't think Gouin even saw them. It was June 10, 1970.

4

Never have I seen such thickets of personal papers in one place. Robert couldn't have written all that much – a more assiduous writer would certainly have produced much more. But Robert kept everything. When computers appeared, he would have none of them, of course. There were ideas scrawled on restaurant placemats, on paper napkins even. Two minuscule verses on a matchbook. Poetry on the backs of bills, on balled-up sheets pulled out of recycling boxes – typical hackneyed mad-genius writer shit, overflowing every room and into the hallway. The first time I went over, he explained his filing system, along with details and digressions, some entirely incoherent, about his various periods and influences and the encounters that had shaped him and made him so productive. He talked fast and was excited enough to make it clear that by crossing the threshold of his apartment I had pierced a hole in the dyke. 'Over there are my eight-syllable works, then the nines and the tens. Here are my alexandrines. Experimental verse forms.' He took out a pad and opened to a random page: ten-line stanzas, the first with lines of four, five, six, seven, eight, nine, ten, eleven, twelve and then thirteen feet, in an ABCDE-FGHIJ pattern; in the next each line had an additional foot, rhymed BCDEFGHIJK, and so on, until the tenth strophe. At first glance the rhymes seemed to work. From a metrical standpoint, he was liberal with the syneresis and the silent e's. In one spot the tottering piles, noticeably smaller than the others, constituted his South American period. ('Are you familiar with Pablo Neruda?') Then there were the many subgenres of the last three decades, his Montreal years. 'Solid stuff, at least a poem a day, up to ten if I don't drink too much. And my thoughts. You know, like a scattered diary. If for some reason I didn't write a poem one day, well, that meant two the day after. My record is thirty-six. In a single day!' Robert brandished a desk lamp as far as its cord would stretch to show me, in the corner of his closet, the four sheets with a cross-shaped fold that he had filled at lumber camp. Beside these relics the proliferation had overgrown the closet and piled up as high as my waist in the middle of the room, as tall as a man in the corners. Together these piles formed a labyrinth through which you could travel from the door to each piece of furniture, to the bed and the kitchen table and the living room couch, in front of which a thirteen-inch TV was ensconced in a wall of papers. In among the pads and loose pages were all manner of books, poetry collections, encyclo-pedias of esoterica, supermarket gossip mags and pulpy paperbacks destabilizing towers I feared to touch.

To increase the capacity of his archive, Robert acquired bunkbeds. The top bunk was piled to the ceiling with masses of newspapers and booklets; to accommodate even more, he had sawed the wooden posts, reducing the height between the bottom mattress and the top bunk to a narrow crevice he could wiggle into. He'd stopped turning on the heat years ago – the mountains of paper in front of the baseboards were a fire hazard. Because he was on the second floor of a three-storey building, Robert claimed, the downstairs neighbours heated his apartment. The truth was that, even under four blankets, he started freezing his ass off every year in late October. The window frame was wood and must have been from the forties; flowers of mould grew happily in its warped frame, and the pane was covered over with a multicoloured frost that gained a half-inch in thickness as winter wore on. He often slept on the couch, where it was warmer. During the last winter he spent at home, I tried to help him keep the drafts out by sticking plastic film over the window. It wasn't easy to do without knocking over the piles of papers rising up to the middle of the window. The plastic clung tight, like a reefed sail filled by the draft slipping in from the street; you could see it breathe when the door opened and shut. Then the bottom came unstuck and it swayed in the cold air, like a sheet drying on a clothesline.

I could never quite shake the feeling that I was using Robert. Who knows what would have become of my own writing under different circumstances; no one can say what life had in store to the right once we've turned left. I probably would have started writing again anyway, without Robert. I would have found another way. But he was the one I settled on, and I squeezed all the juice I could from him. I was also the only one who stood by him to the very end. There was no family. His brother Yves had been dead over fifteen years. His nieces and nephews knew nothing about their uncle, just a few stories of his wandering and his craziness. He was a ghost nicknamed after a low-grade facsimile, grown so diaphanous you could see the blood in the veins in his hands. He'd also grown diffuse, as much in his words as his physical presence: as he moved through the smoke you could barely see him, just the plume rising from his head like a pair of antlers. That smoke had saturated his apartment. The piles of papers and yellowed notebooks all smelled like cold ashtrays, and no sooner were the dishrags wet than they began to reek of socks worn two weeks, impregnating plates and glasses with the odour of dried urine.

It wasn't friendship that took me to see Robert. My attraction was nothing more than selfish, morbid curiosity. It came as a huge surprise to me. I don't make friends with many people, and I am not drawn to eccentrics. I wanted to make him talk. The second time we met, and the first time we drank together, after leaving the Poetry Van and the poets in the park, gave me a sense that I was in the presence of a living treasure, a man whose experience and advice would guide me, a writing mentor who would restore the touch I'd lost when my children were born, and again at the onset of my anxiety when my book was published. He'd help me rediscover the abandon of writing for its own sake. When he let me read his archives, what I found there was the thing itself, writing, a stubborn impulse that survived under any circumstance, because it had to. The texts themselves were meagre pickings, barely salvageable first drafts. Just plain bad, really: even as a fellow failed poet, I couldn't find another way to slice it. Robert wouldn't be my writing godfather. He spun a good yarn, had a gift for making things up, or maybe a tendency to stray from the truth – you could tell by the sparkle in the corner of his squinty eye as he let out a big puff of smoke. I'd found a clown, a character, a subject to objectify.

After we'd hung out several times, I realized he'd become much more than that. One night he coughed so hard he threw up a mixture of beer, bile and blood. After I helped him get up and walk to the living room, he thanked me. There was no pride, just gratitude, and he opened up a bit. He had cancer. Without me and the joints I rolled for him (enough to recover the technique I'd long forgotten), he told me he would never make it through the surges of pain. He'd always hidden his true self behind a character; now it was being revealed to me. He cut the shit after that, just a little. I couldn't quite laugh with him in the same way. Nor could I pity him. This was bigger than me now. I was his friend.

The summer we met we just followed the Poetry Van around town. No need to call each other to set a meeting – the crew who ran that show, the Disembodied Poets, would handle our schedules. I could tell from these first evenings that Robert enjoyed cutting a ghostlike figure. He always sat at the back, but plenty of people knew who Baloney was. He was living out his reputation as a has-been, coasting on a career he'd never had. The oldest among them had been running into him for twenty-five years, in back alleys ('where all the best lines hide') and at second-tier events; he was a co-founder of the seminal magazine *Dog Food* (you'll find his name in the small print of Issue No. 1.); he'd been in the same bar, at one point or another, with everyone who'd ever dreamed of wielding a pen. I did a little research. There were crumbs here and there, on various websites – a long anonymous bibliography without a title, let alone a system; a study of zines and self-publishing; a PhD student's investigations of the ersatz remainders of the counterculture. Robert had three chapbooks to his name, all published in Montreal by Éditions Gratte-Q: *Calvapasse* (1992), *Stroboscrape* (1993) and *Lorraine lumière* (1995). Needless to say, he couldn't show me a single copy. He'd burned them long ago, he said, in a solemn rite of purification. Other Éditions Gratte-Q titles were equally hard to come by. I even checked L'Incunable, that cavernous bookstore with a hazy, pungent backroom on Rue Ontario. Jack told me he'd stocked the first two titles when they came out, but they'd been impossible to find for a long time.

On our third meeting I began to notice the old poets, some of whom had been fairly important in their day, coming up to Robert to say hi. I decided to keep a low profile. They intimidated me, and no one ever remembered me, I was a nobody here. I felt weird about my interest in Robert and didn't want to be noticed. But I couldn't help myself. I was drawn to him by the same attraction that pulls us back to a new lover, a curiosity that takes us out of ourselves and makes us behave in ways we otherwise wouldn't – a gratuitous act with no guaranteed outcome. Sure, they were friendly, but the poets didn't stick around talking to Baloney any longer than they had to. Their discussions quickly turned to absurdities and puns. At that point, what I wanted was to listen to him talk, and these evenings weren't ideal for that: it would be getting late by the time we set off for the tavern or his apartment on Langelier, a fair distance from the Metro. I realized we would have to see each other more than once a month, without so many distractions. But these visits were enough for our ties to take. You can't become part of someone else's life without a few complications.

5

He dreamed of monsters coming over the horizon, straddling mountaintops the way you pull yourself out of a pool, arms first, then a leg. Perched there like vultures, they looked out in his direction, watching for the signal to traverse the plains in four strides and lay waste to everything in sight. But they just stayed put, glued to the mountains, foaming at the mouth, growling and uprooting trees by the handful as easily as clumps of moss. With giant talons they crumbled mountaintops like cornbread; spurred on by their own applause, they crushed one after another, sending whole rock faces hurtling down like grains of sand. Their growling mixed in with explosions, muffled by stone walls and muted by distance, reverberating through the valley before reaching him a few seconds later. It sounded like a nearby village being strafed on a summer night, all quiet but for the irregular blasts of faraway bombs, that moment you suddenly understand, in a shelter that can do nothing to protect you, that it will all be over soon.

Robert awoke to a sharp tap on the sheet metal inches above his head. Was some all-powerful demon showering him with mountain gravel from great heights? Or was it just Luis, throwing rocks to fuck with him? He raised his chest and propped himself up on his elbows. There was no way to sit up without hitting his head on the diagonal wall of this lean-to he slept in, a stump of wood and warped metal jutting out from the side of a stable like a mushroom next to the rusted-out carcass of a car. It had been a doghouse until the dog died and wasn't replaced. Then it had been a tool shed for a while, and Robert moved in after Luis kicked him out of the volunteers' shed.

It was a dark, hot night that should have been glassy and moonless like all the rest but wasn't. The cattle were shuffling around their pen, not far from the stable, kicking up dust that filled the air and nostrils. A cow's lowing leapt an octave. Robert closed his eyelids, then opened them, to compare degrees of darkness. Inside and out were one and the same. He pressed his index fingers down on his eyeballs – they were hard to the touch, and he felt tiny shocks on his retinas, and kept pushing on his closed eyes a few seconds longer for the novelty of seeing circles in the darkness, circles rolling to the left when he pushed them to the right. Stretched out with his bundle tucked under his head, he heard the distant rumble roaring over the valley as the monsters pulverized another summit. The sheet metal started clattering again. No, not stones: it sounded not like a cracked cymbal, more like a bell damped by a hand, striking ever faster and over and over and over. After a moment of disbelief he understood: it was raining on his lean-to. Which meant it must be raining on the stable, pouring down on the fields and on the animals and over the entire hacienda. The plantation was drinking up the moisture that would save it from drying up completely. The toughest of the cows would be saved. He searched for his lighter in the bundle, but came up only with a pencil and a candle stub in among loose sheets of paper and clothing. The water was dripping in along the slant of the metal roof, slowly being imbibed by the sand on the ground. Robert listened to the falling drops for a long time, eyes open, in darkness sporadically shot through by lightning. He reached through the opening between the plank wall and the ground and turned his palm skyward.

For the first time since settling here, water was coming to him. How many gallons had he drawn from the well and then hauled through the fields to the drinking troughs? No one had counted. How many drops had overflowed the rims of the twin buckets held by a crooked pole that left a callus the size of a ten-peso coin on his seventh cervical vertebra, only to evaporate the second they hit the ground? No one knew. The earth kept no records. Between the slats of his hovel, the lightning appeared a few seconds ahead of the unsounded rumbling. The mountain and valley were under attack, not by the gringos or ancient Maya resurrected, but by the elements that had been biding their time since he washed up here, far off the map in deepest Mexico. The hacienda had been losing the battle to drought. Thanks to this storm, it might survive a little longer. This new beginning would be celebrated by Don Alejandro, prancing around in his insufferable *charro* getup. He'd probably invite the mariachi band from town. Young Nahua women would come down from the mountain to dance in a garland-festooned courtyard. They'd chase decapitated cocks, a few young farmers would announce their betrothal, and Doña María would insist that one and all give praise to the Señor, out loud and at length, for this deluge.

The miraculous hammering on the metal convinced Robert to get out. An event of such rarity, sure to go down in the history of the region, a milestone in the lives of all who experienced it, demanded more from him than lying in the mud of his hovel observing grey flashes through the rotting planks. His bundle was soaked but it held nothing of consequence beyond a pouch of tobacco and a few sheets of paper. Robert remembered every word he had written. And he'd managed to mail his last notebook to Yves a few weeks earlier. Seven times he had handed over a bundle of change and a full notebook addressed to his brother, in exchange for a virgin replacement, to the pedlar who delivered mail to the hacienda in a busted-up truck. These regular packages were the one way Robert had to maintain some semblance of a sense of time. Two pages a day. One hundred and ninety-six per notebook. He must have been working at the Ordoñezes' foundering ranch for two years. The volunteers called him Perdito. Luis, the foreman, knew he was wasn't worth his salt, but had told Robert the other volunteers all believed in his talent because he never stopped writing except when he was working. They all listened in respectful silence to the poems he recited in his incomprehensible language while they walked side by side through the rows of corn, or washed the cattle, or patched the roofs, or drove posts for a new enclosure.

Robert stood upright under the vertical downpour, hair pressed down over his face, oily wet-dog smell steaming from his beard, feet slopping around in sand-filled, waterlogged leather sandals. On clear days you could see miles down the valley into the western mountains below, normally dark-hued, but orange when the sun obliged. Under a full moon you could walk without a lantern and watch the sorrels standing in the pasture land like sandstone statues, their stillness troubled only by the occasional flick of a tail. He knew the stable was intact. So was the wall encircling the hacienda and main outbuilding; he could see them in the lightning. But the mountains had disappeared, and in the flashes you could just barely make out the cattle in the pens below, huddling close to shield themselves from the apocalypse. The lightning was striking with increasing violence and frequency. Wind rose up to buffet the columns of rain. Now the lightning hit right in front of him, and Robert couldn't hear his own cries as he was thrown back. It had surely been drawn by the lone tree two hundred paces off, in the middle of the field, where the farmhands gathered for their afternoon siesta. He closed his eyes and imagined the tree ripped top to bottom by a sawmill, black and smouldering as each half split away like an error, the charred bodies of sleepers clinging to its roots. The raindrops were spanking the top of his skull and his shoulders with improbable force, he thought, as he lifted his chin, face-up to the night. Behind his eyelids he felt new electrical shocks, this time a kaleidoscope of colours and formless blobs swallowing each other and spitting each other out, and then everything turned momentarily red when a new round of lightning cleaned the slate. It was spectacular, despite the pain every drop inflicted on his eyes and his face chapped by salt and burnt by the perpetual sun. Sepia-toned memories flooded back – a viscous belt fight between his cousin Jean-Claude and a bully, swimming in the lake on the other side of Mount Tremblant, a broken limb splayed at ninety degrees, sugar loaves melting on a sideboard, Denis in the emptiness of the forest, a baker pulling a putrid pie from the oven, Simon unable to sketch the repulsive face of an American woman with a swollen goitre and enucleated eyes, and then spiders, spiders by the dozen in the yellow jungle.

The din changed in tone: in place of the muffled sound of rain on earth was a percussive splattering of heavy rain on pooled water. In daylight he could have *seen* the grime dripping off his sweaty, dusty clothing, seen the filth and stench he no longer even noticed wrung from his clothes, light garments grown so heavy with the water, clinging to his body like a new skin grown over an older one ravaged by sun. His bundle hung from his hand like a saturated sponge. A stream as thick as his wrist poured forth. He let it drop. With his face still angled toward the sky, eyes closed, mouth open, he raised his arms and spread them into a cross, the better to feel every drop pricking his wrists, then little by little he reached up toward the source of the water, as high as he could, to feel the water sooner.

Years earlier, with water whipping his head and an eddy swirling around his feet, he had been caught off guard by an explosion. His comrades were unarmed, as far as he knew, and he trusted them. They hadn't seen other people for days. With arms upraised, momentarily stunned by the sun and the water on his face, he turned around slowly and saw Simon floating naked, face down, swaying in the current. Leandro and Raúl were still as statues on the riverbank in front of four assholes in military peacoats pointing their machine guns and barking orders. No one noticed when Robert pissed himself. He wanted to walk up to Simon, to turn him onto his back, but two of the men stepped forward, feet in the water now, and started yelling even louder. Robert got out of the swimming hole, buck naked, and joined his friends with guns pointed at their chests.

While one man searched their bags and the pockets of the clothes they had thrown on the ground, another spat questions at Leandro, punctuated with thrusts of his gun. Robert looked at Simon – hair and arms, ass and heels sticking out of the water, still-raw lines inscribed on his back by the thicket they got caught in the previous day. He'd torn his jacket and swore his head off while the others laughed at him. For the first time, Robert noticed how thin his friend had become. He pictured them in Sherbrooke, in what felt like another century, drunkenly stumbling in each other's arms in the Wellington Street slush. The waterfall's eddy gently pulled the body toward the edge of the pool. Ripples, ferns and roots troubled the surface; blood coloured the water. If he hadn't been killed instantly, Simon would surely have drowned, unconsciously perhaps, without suffering, one hoped. How could this have happened? Why was Leandro, their peace-loving friend and leader of this trip since they met at a Lima café, now lying on the ground, held by his hair with a pistol at his throat? There was no clear or easy explanation. Robert had no plea to make. Even if his Spanish were up to the task, it wouldn't have registered through his moans and sobs. The man searching their bags alerted the leader. He'd found a volume of Octavio Paz, a bilingual Neruda, some notebooks and a small red-bound volume in a foreign language. They were yelling now, pressing Raúl's face against a book held open on the ground, like you would shove a puppy's nose in its urine to teach it a lesson. The leader came toward Robert to force him to hurry up and get dressed. One of the men leaned toward the body, grabbed on to a foot, dragged it to the water's edge and flipped it over. You couldn't recognize the mud-splattered face, the beard clumped with dirt, the mess covering his chest – there was no way to find the black hole, the blood and guts, the digested matter, the bones, the light, the hope. The leader held Robert at gunpoint, while his free hand pointed toward the bags, the body and Leandro; he bombarded Robert with questions that would more likely have yielded answers if he'd slowed down and addressed him like a child. Robert kept repeating the same phrases: *habla francés, habla francés, canadiense francés*. Leandro stood up again. They let him speak. After a few sentences the leader came toward Robert and pushed him in the back, toward Peru, suggesting he be on his way. Leandro also pointed north. The men picked up the books, bags and clothing and walked off in the opposite direction in single file: three in front and the fourth behind Raúl and Leandro. They left Simon's body lying there, cock out, skin covered in mud, arms spread over his head, hand in the water. For a second Robert thought he should die right here with his friend. But the voices rose up again, muffled by the vegetation, and his instinct told him he'd be better off dying somewhere else.

Robert was not the first drifter to wash up, half-naked and half-dead, at the gate of the Ordoñez hacienda. Usually they were sent on their way, the fortunate ones after a glass of milk and a tortilla, which Doña María saw as down payment on her afterlife. No matter how tanned he'd become in years of wandering, Robert still didn't look like a native. His inability to understand a word they said made him all the more intriguing to the people who chose to swing open the metal gate for him. Luis put Robert on a mule to take him to an outbuilding, but he immediately fell face forward onto the animal's mane. It was months before he could marshal the rudimentary Spanish Doña María taught him in the evenings after chores to tell his story. He explained who he was and how he had got there, keeping it vague and allusive. The road that brought him to Mexico in midsummer was a long one, a convoluted journey that had begun in an unseasonably warm mid-September in the Andes. So warm, on the Chile–Peru border, that he and Simon had decided to cool off in the waterfall where his friend's body probably lay to this day, unless the animals had pecked and dragged it miles away, over rocky ground, or his murderers had returned to clean up. Wherever his bodily remains were now, they were surely decomposed – it had been two years, or three even, now that Robert stood here all alone in the eye of a storm that seemed to be rinsing his memories, leaving them rubbed smooth and eroded like stone blades unearthed by accident, artefacts whose original shape one could only guess at.

As he'd fled north back to Peru, away from the waterfall, out of breath and in a state of panic, images of the previous days played back in his head. There was the thicket where Simon had scratched up his back (broken branches, young shoots crushed under his weight). The rectangle of earth tamped down by their tents over three days was seared in his memory for the first few miles of his walk; he remembered the winged beast they had roasted on a spit along with scorched lizards, cans of beans and ears of corn. He recalled the jokes Leandro (or Simon?) had made, riding him about the moustache on the prostitute he'd slept with the night before they left for Chile. Then came forests, luminous nights and sunless noons, erratic gunfire in the distance, the coolness that came above a certain altitude, low-hanging fruit he gathered – the memories were a jumble, until he joined the Quechua caravan of people and donkeys bearing baskets. With no energy left and no shoes on his feet, he looked frightful when they reached Lima. There was a Canadian embassy, but with no papers or money, the staff would surely shut the door in his face. Who would believe his story? He'd be beaten and sold to the local police. He pictured them in feathered headdresses, bleeding him dry on a cold slab in some basement room with stone walls lit only by torches. Yelling to be heard over the crowd of people gathered for the sacrifice, they'd interrogate him about the disappearance of Leandro Flores, last seen a few weeks earlier in a motel in the company of two foreigners. All over town he imagined he saw posters: Leandro's and Raúl's faces riddled with holes, Simon's in a state of decomposition, a mere skull with patches of beard peeling off, green skin, eyes hanging from sockets.

Then: alleyways, skinned dogs, garbage-can chicken bones. Robert woke up in places where he hadn't gone to sleep, washed dishes and scrubbed toilets in a sorry dive, stowed away in the back of a truck headed up the coast, got to know the narrow alleys of Quito, which resembled those of Lima, as the back streets of Bogotá differed little from those of Managua. Laconic strangers guided him through jungles where he feared falling asleep lest he be attacked by a striped snake or puma-sized tarantula with glow-in-the-dark eyes, creatures that would like nothing more than to crack his skull and suck out his brains. In Panama, he saw a man stabbed with a decisive thrust above the navel, followed by ten more once he keeled over. In a smaller city further north, he found a trash-strewn stretch of sand next to a concrete wall separating the beach from a slum, and a giant crumbling boardwalk. Or maybe it was a dock, who knows, Robert couldn't even say for sure which ocean it was. The sun rose and set, but it was hard to ascertain exactly where. The only direction that now mattered was away from hunger. The godforsaken alleys near the wall provided enough to entice him to stay for a while.

He spent a few nights under a torn orange tarp, days watching unremitting waves churning bits of plastic whose origin he never determined, cracked buoys and seaweed and rotten fish that conjured up images of Simon's corpse, suspended at the crest of a somersault while an eel wriggled into his mouth, only to emerge from his eye socket and be swept away by the undertow, disappearing amid the debris jockeying for position at the surface. His respite came to an abrupt end when Robert was chased away by a local gang. They didn't understand a word of his demented ramblings, but the tape-handled shards of glass they used as shivs clearly asserted their prior claim to this turf. He climbed aboard a chicken bus, with kids standing on the shocks and hanging from windows, the better to push the rooftop cages back into place when they slid. After three hours of severe discomfort, caught in a traffic jam, he had to leap off and urgently find a spot to expel the diarrhea that prevented him from taking anything but tiny stiff steps. A garbage can would have done the trick, but he lucked into the dressing room of a marble-columned public bathhouse, where he basked in the luxury of shitting on a toilet and then took a lengthy shower, scraping out the paper and crud clumped in his crack hairs and washing the accumulated grime from his body. He deep-scrubbed his armpits, smelling his fingers in the hope that the odour had dispersed. He hadn't washed in weeks. His clothes on the dressing room bench were resplendently filthy and ripe with piss and shit. He turned around to face the wall, put his hands on either side of the showerhead and lifted up his face toward the jet of clean water, experiencing each and every drop, water dripping like time. He forgot who and where he was and why he had no feeling in his stomach, despite the tight ball in his throat.

Robert cried out when he felt a hand on his shoulder. Dawn was bursting through the darkness, but it still took a moment to recognize Luis in the blur of the downpour. The foreman shoved him in the back and yelled at him to move his ass. The hacienda and its outbuildings stood on high ground, but the downward slope below was alive with rivulets of muddy water flowing toward the fields and pooling in the animals' pens. Stunned cattle were floundering; the two calves were in it up to their bellies and bucking their heads, jumping up and trying to extricate their hooves from the sty, as if to find a foothold to stand upright on two legs. Maybe the trampling cattle had eroded the dusty soil over the years. Maybe it was a natural basin that no one had noticed, in the absence of midnight mudslides. Maybe the monsters, instead of crossing the plain in three or four steps, preferred to move forward by excavating canals, and a great chasm would open up any moment to swallow up the pens and the fields and the entire hacienda.

Robert saw Luis and the others scrambling out of the shed in their underwear, waving arms and crying for help in an attempt to save the cattle, their movements fixed like photographs by the white lightning. The men pushed the cows toward the gate of the pen, dragged the calves by their necks toward the top of the slope. There was slipping and sliding, mooing and swearing. Robert followed them along the stable, behind his lean-to, beside the old car with broken fragments of windshield scattered over lacerated bench seats erupting with stuffing and springs. Unmoored parts and wires dangled under the hood.

The tires were flat, the mirrors cracked. Simon couldn't believe his eyes. The fucking bastards. The Valiant sputtered and coughed. She should have had a few thousand miles in her before packing it in. True, they'd had a good run up to now by steering clear of problems and the people who attracted them: small men with big mouths, dealers, tripped-out hippies, overly attractive women. After they'd made it this far on luck, or maybe chance, here was the proverbial shit coming in to land on their faces.

Their first months on the road were, hands down, the best of Robert's life. October was the apex: after crossing the States, they'd pitched tents in Yosemite with Eileen and Barbara, who they'd picked up in Illinois, on their way to Oregon. There followed a glorious month of non-stop fucking and cheap wine and copious reefer and spectacular nature, enough to make them all aware of their own insignificance in the grand scheme of things. When the women went on their way, Simon and Robert were left alone with sex on the brain. They experimented a little, unsuccessfully, and never mentioned it again. They drove on to Flagstaff, Arizona, where they now found themselves in the parking lot of a bar, staring at Simon's smashed-up Valiant. It must have been the two little punks who'd turned surly when they lost at pool. They'd taken off. At least things wouldn't escalate. But it was high time to leave this meretricious town, pretty as a picture but rotten on the inside, where they now had enemies. They walked to the hotel. Simon called his dad the next day; the day after, they were on an airplane to Ecuador.

Quito was a thousand times poorer than anything they'd ever seen, and infinitely more raw. It became their base, a place to come back to after excursions around Ecuador and Colombia. They rented a room for what felt like a pittance but was more like a fortune, in the house of a small business-man who said he loved North Americans and sang snatches of Elvis Presley with lyrics of his own invention. Until they met Leandro and Raúl, they whiled away the hours on the wicker benches in front of the house, well-supplied with books, fruit and notebooks, writing poems and reciting them to amused passersby. The women always slipped by quickly, with baskets of bananas in their arms and naked children running around their legs. Farmers walked down the middle of the road with their animals, who were mostly docile but sometimes put up a fight by pulling on their choke ropes.

Determined to help, Robert gave the fattest of the cows (who was still pretty scrawny) a shove on the ass, but it slipped in the water and refused to go into the barn. When Luis pulled, it locked its knees and its hooves furrowed the ground. Robert slid and fell face down in the mud. Down below in the pen that had turned into a lake, the others were wrestling with the animals. A light went on in the window of the hacienda's big house. Don Alejandro appeared, arms waving. As he came closer, Robert feared the man might talk to him.

Simon held out their passports. Three months of vacation in the Adirondacks, no more. They revved up the Valiant and crossed the border.

Robert examined his surroundings. It was definitely morning, the sandstone ashen after the storm. Time to go home. His bundle had slid down the hill – he saw it floating in the pool, pulled in wide circles by the slow current. He said goodbye to it all and started walking north.

6

I'd seen death before. This I can say without hyperbole:
it wasn't like a person or animal you spend a little time
with at the very end, watching them suffer but always
from a distance, until the news comes down that their story
is over while yours will go on. No, I'd seen the thing itself.
The final exhale after the breath gradually slows down. Lips
that stop trembling, a chest completely still at the end of an
unconscious battle, a head tilted with its eyes rolled back,
breath like a browning apple core, the shrivelled body of a
mummy exhumed from a stone stela.

It was my grandfather. Or what little remained of the man
he had once been. We gathered at his side, summoned by
nurses familiar with the smells of fruits. My mother, sisters,
uncles, aunts and cousins all stayed there with him until his
cerebellum gave out, in the thirty-five-degree July heat

cooled by a fan the size of a large gong. There were long periods of peace, even a few smiles; it seemed as if the light had changed. Someone suggested it might be the soul in transit. It was just us, noticing the room's light.

As Robert and I grew closer and I watched him waste away, it dawned on me that I would be witnessing another death or, worse, end up discovering his cold dead body. Leaving the apartment had become increasingly painful for him. He had his line, 'It's nothing a good toke won't fix,' but I could tell that deep down he was furious he could no longer drink his fill, on account of the stomach ulcers that had showed up when he started popping codeine pills stamped with clovers, checkerboards and women's silhouettes. Sometimes when we went out to eat, he'd go to the bathroom and never come back. In early December he didn't show up to one of our meetings. I called him; no answer. I could have just gone home, or stopped by the following day to suggest another meeting, but I had a feeling this might be it, so I went to his apartment. The door was unlocked. Inside it was dim and silent: no agitated landlord, no cops called in by neighbours complaining of a rotten smell. I pushed the door open and walked in slowly, covering my nose and mouth as a precaution. Other than the grease and cold cigarette smoke, the only smell was my own bad breath.

Robert's entire neolyric period was strewn over the floor. Some of the piles were high enough to conceal a body. I called out and was greeted by silence. The fridge door was open, letting out a wan light that gave a semblance of form to the table, chair, counter and more structurally sound piles of papers. In the bedroom, lit only by the hall light, a decade of fallen prose had formed a large mound from which a bare foot emerged. I turned on the ceiling light and tried to step over the papers. I slipped. Robert lay buried under his poems, on his stomach, arms open, head to one side. He'd shat himself and wore an expression of terror, like a man who'd seen Medusa pass by without daring to raise his eyes. The shallow breaths he took every five seconds weren't drawing enough air to fill his lungs. I crouched down next to him. His breath stank worse than mine. He didn't move his eyes, but his mouth, toothless as a moray eel and stretched by suffering, managed to produce a whisper. 'Okay, that's enough, buddy.'

In his palliative-care bed at Maisonneuve-Rosemont Hospital, where *Cancer* had been stamped on his record, and where cancer would see the process of decay through until it reached his cerebellum, Robert fell asleep with a tube in his nose and one in his urethra. I went home with his key in my pocket, and when I passed strangers in the street, people I didn't know and didn't want to, rotten and ugly like Robert, like me and Joannie, like Jasmin and Chloé, whose childhood grace period would one day elapse, I took comfort in the thought that I would never lay eyes on any of these repellent creatures again, and that was just fine, thank you very much.

In the days that followed, it fell to me to contact what family Robert had. I wasn't aware of any last wishes. A will definitely wasn't his style, though I had a private laugh at the thought of Robert at the notary's office, bolt upright with his hands on his knees and a fifty-yard stare, handing down instructions for his personal archives in a torrent of circumvolutions and obscenities. I imagined it would take hours to unearth an address book in the chaos of his apartment, but there it lay, next to the phone, like the handiest of daily tools. More like an ironic symbol of his solitude: it contained exactly two numbers, mine and Yves's, which was crossed out and replaced by Yves's son's. After expressing sadness at his uncle's condition, and astonishment at my affection for Robert, he asked me to keep him posted on any progress.

I decided to give myself no choice: I'd accompany Robert to the very end, as best I could. I visited him at the hospital every other day, straightened up his piles of verse (without checking dates), cleaned up the messes in his apartment – certain pages were soaked in urine – and brought him a half-empty notebook selected at random. If the hospital drugs had left a corner of his mind intact, he just might write a little more, to keep fighting off those moments of nothingness. I admit I didn't feel strong enough to help him clean himself, as he asked once. I made sure he got something to eat beyond the bland hospital stews. Not that he ever cared about food – he happily ate the same thing every day: ground beef and potatoes he fried up or whatever he ordered in from the corner diner. I preferred to get takeout and bring it myself, to alleviate the feeling that I wasn't doing anything.

I was seeing Robert often and coming home atrophied, and Joannie was sick of it. Was I not enjoying the luxury of chatting away, about writing no less, with a worthless, disgusting old man? She was only half-right about Robert. The rest was accurate. She and I had life depending on us: two little unformed lives crawling all over and pleading for help the only way they knew how, by crying and throwing everything on the ground. I had to do my part. After looming on the horizon for months, Christmas was now upon us, sirens blazing. Like every year, we'd spend two weeks with Joannie's family. Robert said *yeah, yeah* with his eyes and shooed me away with his hands, as if he were flicking crumbs under his bed. But I wasn't asking permission. I had come to regretfully inform him that I was abandoning him.

There's no shortage of reasons to hate Christmas. But that year I didn't let it get to me. There are times when sadness overcomes all else, and we have no choice but to burrow deep into it and dig up whatever it is we need to enjoy ourselves. We stayed in the Bois-Francs, where the snow alternated with rain. We drank too much and laughed just enough. The photos religiously checked on the little screen after every exposure revealed how far my hairline had receded in the year we were putting behind us, and how your eyes betray the smiles you fake. As the sole next of kin, I'd left my phone number with the hospital staff. They didn't call.

7

During the entire trip, Robert contacted one person only, and indirectly: the notebooks he mailed his brother Yves were his sole proof of life. As for what kind of life it was, Robert could no longer say for sure. At the Canadian embassy in Mexico City, they first shut the door but eventually relented, annoyed by his insistence, and dug up a Franco-Manitoban secretary who could identify the accent he used to talk nonsense. After interrogations and hours of investigations deep within the bowels of the embassy, they let Robert phone Simon's father. Hours spent waiting alone in a room furnished only with a table, chair and broken coffeemaker caused Robert to start doubting his own story. Maybe he was no longer alive. Maybe everything that had happened since the gunshots in the waterfall was the contrivance of puppeteers who took pleasure in toying with the mind of an unbeliever held captive in purgatory. His voice was much higher-pitched in French than in his garbled English and Spanish, as if the words came from someone else, an acquaintance he hadn't heard from in ages. After four short sentences attempting to explain what had happened, silence set in. It lasted a minute, or maybe an hour. Finally Simon's father spoke. 'Yeah, I figured you boys were dead.' He sent money and agreed to stand guarantor for the papers required to travel between worlds. Robert was allowed to wash, shave and dress. One fall morning in 1976, he got off a plane at Mirabel and onto a staircase wheeled out for him alone.

The days that followed took him from motel room to motel room, until he got off a bus in Sherbrooke. Everything was made of different materials now. He had to stop himself from touching the walls to make sure, but from their look alone he could tell they would disintegrate in his hand like vanilla mousse. Like all old people tested by adversity, Simon's father now looked his age. In another empty room, with a table and three chairs but no coffee machine, he sat with Robert, who retold the story of his friend's death to a low-ranking police officer. They came back later that week to meet with another man who, even in his civvies, was unmistakably important. In the blasé tone of someone who has seen it all before, he told them a joint investigation would be opened with the Chilean authorities. This late in the game, and with such fragmentary information, they shouldn't get their hopes up for repatriating the body. There were further phrases and condolences. The old man could have blamed Robert for taking so long to come home, for not contacting him immediately, but he was too weighed down by grief to let hatred get the better of him. Robert was now a pitiful wreck. He looked much older than he was, and he wore an empty stare. It would have been far too easy for Dr. Alphonse Saint-Amand to crush him like an ant, but that would have undermined the dignity he was striving so hard to maintain through this ordeal.

As he walked into the church for the service, Robert again doubted whether he was actually alive. He sat alone in the last pew. There were other people he knew – his colleague from the factory with a halved finger, the former journalist, the director of the university cultural-centre gallery, a few of Simon's rival painters and, of course, Jeannette and Nicole. They were up at the front, with the same bodies, but souls somehow emptied out, like those old-fashioned dolls with rivets for joints that close their eyes when leaned backward. After all these years, one was still plunking baskets of fries down on a counter, while the other delivered her lines in a monotone before being wheeled into the wings on a float. After the homily, the organist produced a squealing coda and the empty casket was borne down the central aisle. Everyone glided in Robert's direction. Some pretended not to see him; others looked right through him. The echoey harmonics made him want to run up to the choir, knock down the priest, stamp on his throat, stick his thumbs in his eyes, yank his robes over his head and take a shit on him, then catch up with the girls and smack them with the altar candles or, better yet, drag them to a King Street bar, get them drunk just like old times and rape them. But they were stronger than he was. They'd fight back, overpower him, break his limbs and cauterize the wounds with burning brands, as payback for the love he'd stolen from them. Slumped over in the bus taking him from the green pastures of Sherbrooke to Montreal's grey concrete, he chuckled when the idea of killing himself occurred to him for the first time. He fought it off, afraid that suicide might bring him back to life.

Robert staggered around a half-drowned city that felt as unfinished as he was, its stadium missing a mast, its young people naively impulsive and stoned blind, until he'd spent the wad of ten-dollar bills Simon's father had thrown in his face as a going-away present, along with a bevy of insults. With no money for a hotel room, he fell back on the Metro, spending his days deep in the city's entrails and his nights on the grates through which warm gusts wafted up from the abyss, sucking what was left out of him.

Time started running again one morning when he saw a man catapulted into the air by a car as he crossed Rue Ontario to catch a bus. After some complex aerial gymnastics, the man smacked into a bus shelter and rolled onto the lawn right in front of him. He had gained extra elbows and lost half his face. The man gurgled awhile, then stopped moving altogether, with one hand covering his eyes and the other behind his head, like someone settling onto a couch for a nap. Robert noticed just how exhausted he was. He'd had enough. It was time to do something, anything. He picked up his bag and split before the curious onlookers showed up.

That very day he shaved in a restaurant bathroom and bought new clothes with the proceeds of a stolen Betamax. The next day he got an under-the-table job as a dépanneur deliveryman and took a room in a scuzzy boarding house. A year later he was hired by the City of Montreal. For next to nothing he rented a two-bedroom apartment in one of the hives that line Boulevard Langelier. It was spring 1980. Robert's wandering years were over. In exchange for days spent cleaning the change rooms of a public pool, he'd sleep under the same roof every night. He decided to enjoy the course now set in motion, to see this return to the comfort he'd known before his southern escapade as a victory. Life was even sweeter now. With union wages, Robert was rolling in money. He bought a TV, started washing in hot water several times a week, got back in touch with Yves. The same cars, faces and old buildings rolled by in an infinite loop that contradicted the promise of linearity held out by the calendars inside his cigarette packs. Poetry began to rise again, out of the grime and the change-room gutters he swabbed, out of the gunk in the corners of his eyes and his pushed-back cuticles, the butterflies and the girls with swaying hips he observed from his balcony as they made their way up Langelier toward the Metro station, cracking jokes and singing; it flowed from the old cabinet television with a built-in turntable, smells of decomposing earth and memories welling up in him from deep in the backcountry. He bought poetry collections and stocked up on virgin notebooks. Simon was still dead and still at Robert's side, like an excrescence bigger and better-looking and more present than himself, casting a shadow on every inanimate object and living creature around him: a favourite lighter disappeared; a fling with a neighbour soured to the point of threats, until she had to move; pens dried up and with them the flow of poesy, to return only months later, though Robert kept writing in the interim, with a pencil, because a body in motion stays in motion.

The same patterns repeated, broken only rarely by surprises. Robert began to actively seek out and enact the unexpected as a way of distracting himself from the death wish that came back the moment he got used to having a dry place to sleep. One spring, a spider that inhabited a corner of his bedroom ceiling decided, after a one-week trial period, that it preferred the sliver of space between the dresser and the wall. Until he found it dead that autumn, laid out on its back with legs tucked in to its stomach, Robert caught it flies in the double kitchen window. He would wait until they had almost stopped moving, then toss them into the web. In the alley by his apartment that high school kids used as a short-cut, Robert would place objects and observe what fate had in store for them through his double window. A kicked bag of flour didn't go up in a cloud of fine white powder, as expected, but simply slumped over, disembowelled, leaving behind a brown paste compacted by rain. A metal box with a broken latch languished for days before someone had a look, though he had placed six fifty-dollar bills in a Russian doll inside. A book of poems vanished in the night, only to mysteriously reappear the next morning.

Robert started hanging out at Nul-Part on Hochelaga, where the regulars worked hard to make sure nothing unexpected happened, ever. The same two barflies spat the same vitriol about politicians in the same terms with no regard for what the day's news brought. Each piece of human detritus had its set place: Big Grey next to the bathroom; Aline, Pistou and Boutin at the video lottery terminals; and all the others whose names Robert didn't know, but whose booze-addled faces expressed the same fraternal camaraderie, all members of a community knit tight by a shared determination to always sit in the same place and continually suck from the same tap. The employees – two alternating waitresses, a dealer and a doorman – were not immune from the repetition disease. Every once in a while, a group of guys from the neighbourhood would surprise everyone by coming in to warm up with four or five beers before heading downtown to finish the job. Or a pair of young women in faded jeans, manes held fast with hairspray, would shake the fringes on their jackets to the climax of a Bon Jovi power ballad, leaning on the pool table. Then all eyes would finally look up from their drinks, talk would grind to a halt and everyone would drink a little more. Robert stayed in his slot between the jukebox and the stuffed-animal machine, calmly enjoying these moments of awkwardness, observing the foam settling inside his brown glass bottle.

By the mid-eighties, his routine had hardened into an unbroken, perpetual loop: twenty minutes of acrid coughing, breakfast at Vincent's Subs, bathrooms and floors at the Édouard-Montpetit swimming pool, dinner at New Milano Pizzeria or takeout at home, writing, then the descent into oblivion at the Nul-Part or on his living room couch when the beer started flowing too early and freely.

The catacombs of the swimming pool, where Robert disappeared after completing his above-ground tasks, was a parallel world of dripping pipes and humming boilers, where he could go about his business without fear of encountering hale swimmers, white-collar workers or the public. There weren't too many bugs or rats, and Robert learned to live with them in peace and harmony; after all, his job was to dissuade them, through strategies designed to keep them down below with him, from going upstairs where they might encounter hale swimmers, white-collar workers or the public. When he wasn't exhausted from the previous night's drinking, he would skip his nap and use this subterranean downtime to crank out a few poems. If the words weren't forthcoming, he'd stroll through the concrete rooms in search of a leak to plug or a bolt to tighten. When the synchronized-swimming team practised, he'd smoke and watch them through the porthole, engorged by the upside-down view of this ballet of weightlessness, so gracious above the surface, yet jerky and violent beneath, with open and seemingly dislocated hindquarters and writhing legs and windmilling arms propelling swimmers headfirst to the bottom, bodies pushing off and crashing into each other, upsurges and tapered limbs, suits wedged in cracks, red faces and mouths contorted by the strain. Robert would whack off and bury his semen with a flick of his boot in the dust and sand. He had to act quickly, and had even stockpiled barrels of powdered chlorine to conceal him up to his haunches, because you never really knew when to expect the unexpected. At the rec centre the unexpected usually took the form of puddles of vomit or spots of blood, but anything, really, might send someone off in search of the custodian: a broken window, lunch splatter in the staff-room microwave, a bird that had found a way in and had to be chased out – any break in the routine or tiny panic was Robert's to deal with, restoring the world's hypocritical appearance of order, papering over all evidence of the forces he saw as proof of the invisible, all-encompassing power of poetry, which was at work in all things and at all times, but perceptible only to the poets, a form of potential energy turned kinetic by the labour of a small elect.

He knew he wasn't the only one in Montreal who had the gift. Once his connection to the city was strong enough, Robert answered the call of nostalgia for those wild Sherbrooke nights that was tugging at his heartstrings and gnawing at his gut. It was time to go out and find other poets. Just weekends at first, but once he got to know the bars, cafés and even parks where the poets could be found, in their clans or on their own, he began to venture out mid-week as well. The poets got used to the sight of Robert hanging out in the corner of the barroom or boldly occupying a neighbouring table. It was only a matter of time until they started talking to him, offering him a drink and occasionally an end-of-the-night microphone. He always refused. He wasn't afraid of striking up a conversation with the professionals, but always did so as an amateur, an unpublished poet among the published, slightly star-struck by their power yet covetous of their words, proud just to be there, like a suckerfish hoovering all the blood it can as the current sweeps it along. Soon you could find him not only at the usual haunts and theme nights but also at the poets' parties, and in this fraternity he began to shake off the weight of Simon's aura, which he'd always dragged behind him like a cloud of shadow dogging him through the cigarette smoke and back-alley steam.

When he returned to his chlorine pumps, his table at Vincent's Subs or the bar at the Nul-Part, he could now savour the knowledge of his double life, like a comforting white noise. Who, of all these people around him, could claim to have snorted coke with Denis Vanier? Been punched out by Josée Yvon? Attended the launch party for Paul Chamberland's latest, given Lucien Francoeur manuscript advice, talked to François Charron and Claude Beausoleil? Who had so much as laid eyes on Jacques Brault? Who among them knew who these people were or had even an inkling of their capital importance and, by extension,

Robert's own? The answer, of course, was no one. He relished his low profile, necessary to avoid exciting curiosity and envy. The drinkers at the Nul-Part, the acne-faced lifeguards, the passersby on Boulevard Langelier, the waitresses – none could imagine that all the poetry in the city, the country, the entire universe really, converged on their neighbour, their colleague, their anonymous regular customer, to be brought back to life and born anew in the notebooks piling up in his apartment. Robert's double life was like a cog triumphantly produced, hastily bolted on and now somehow miraculously keeping the machine in motion. The thrill of his life as an underground poet caused him to lose sight, for a few years, of the temptation to take his own life.

It was in Boudreau's kitchen, at these parties, that poetry revealed its loftiest face. The poets' battles in rhyme cracked Robert up, but levity was thrown aside fast for swearing and banging fists in condemnation of the Intimists' insipid doggerel. In this group there was anger in spades, but also cracks the hope could filter through. Even democracy seemed possible again. It was at one of these soirées, long after the deps had closed, that they founded a little magazine called *Dog Food*. In a burst of anti-establishment solidarity, a middle finger thrust in the face of reality, the two founders shared the masthead with everyone present. At another party, a guitarist friend named Michel, who accompanied everyone's verse, wrote a blues song to 'La forêt et la montagne,' one of Robert's Eastern Townships sonnets. Time with his new friends showed Robert ways to improve his own writing. In a matter of months he started sounding like them, except of course much better.

Emulation gave Robert the confidence he'd lacked to finally commit. His first two chapbooks cemented his reputation, within his circle, as a poet of some craft. But when his third came out, Boudreau claimed he recognized lines plucked wholesale from Gilbert Langevin – 'Which unto the galaxies,' 'picked bruised,' 'we find ourselves naked,' 'here evil lurks,' 'Spring in the ocean,' 'Barking with desire,' 'our infinite smiles and innumerable sighs' – they weren't reminiscent, they were identical. You could check the manuscripts: the handwriting was Robert's own, the notes in the margins were as real as the trance he had written them in. There are times when great minds align in perfect synergy and synchrony and tune into the same magical frequencies. The kerfuffle forced Robert to face certain facts. From now on he would only write alone. His work was lost on his contemporaries.

A ringing phone jolted Robert from his writing one Sunday at noon. The shock when the young man on the line came to the end of his story was so great that pins and needles pricked Robert's fingers and a tourniquet clamped his throat. His brother Yves was dead and buried, two months ago now, after patient persecution by a cancer that had worn him down in secret, then finished him off with a full-frontal assault the moment he learned of its existence. The caller was Yves's oldest son. In a robotic voice, he apologized for not telling Robert earlier. He was in charge of liquidating the estate and wanted Robert's permission to get rid of the stacked boxes of papers and notebooks taking up space in the basement of the house in Saint-Donat. Robert paid to have the boxes shipped to him. A few days later they arrived: all the poems he'd written before moving into his apartment on Langelier, from the original four sheets given to him by Denis at lumber camp to the last notebook mailed from the hacienda.

In his cluttered apartment, Robert let himself wallow a few weeks in the grief of his brother's death. Then he realized he'd been thrown a final lifeline. Yves had given him back his life's work. Here it was, assembled in one place, a single indivisible whole. As he reread, his body remembered everything the poems left unsaid, tapping into the black, dead memory where he had stored the pleasant warmth of a May night in Nicole's attic room, where he had first given voice to the dread that almost made him tear his eyes from their sockets. The near-perpetual drunkenness that had marked the work with the romance of its themes, and the rings from glasses and cigarette burns adorning the papers. He wanted to reorganize his texts based on the impressions they summoned forth, to cover the floor with the full spectrum of poetic effect they contained. But, after a few readings, the poems ceased to evoke the same memories. The feeling was increasingly attenuated. Robert began to fear someone had tampered with his documents. Eventually he had to face the fact that he was surely not the same self when he was writing, but a conduit for the voice of some stranger, divine perhaps, maybe even the same puppeteer pulling the strings that held him in limbo. He settled on chronological order by date of composition, to make the job easier for whoever discovered his archive. By the late nineties, he had put his past in order. It took up both bedrooms, the kitchen and half the living room. Now he slid back into his invisible routine: his morning expectoration of chunky phlegm, his vertigo, the tickling deep in his lungs. At the Nul-Part, the shit-talkers of yore weren't on their bar stools anymore. Robert stuck to his hole between the jukebox and the stuffed-animal machine. New regulars had usurped the seats of the old ones, a new batch of ignoramuses who had no idea a major poet was silently drinking his beer in their midst.

As he got deeper into his sixties, Robert wondered whether the life he led was actually more momentous than it seemed, another conspiracy of the occult forces that only poetry could unmask. Who knows, there might be an illegitimate child in the States, maybe Illinois. He might have knocked up Eileen at Yosemite. She would have gone home and had their girl, who would now be a beautiful, brilliant blond, the spitting image of her mother made even more beautiful by the blood of the Lacertes, speaking impeccable French with the sexy accent of cultured Americans. Who knows, she might show up any day to find her long-lost father, guided by the single clue in her possession, a poem he'd given her mother before she disappeared with her friend Barbara, an ode to the sun signed with his real name. Maybe it had been Nicole, nine months after he and Simon headed south, who gave birth to a boy as exceptional as his progenitor, a champion swimmer by now, or a gifted musician, or a great poet like his father. Maybe someone, someday, would befriend Robert and take an interest in his writing, recognize its outstanding quality and publish it, to his posthumous glory.

One afternoon while he was mopping the men's change room, a pain in his chest took Robert by surprise. He awoke in an unfamiliar bed, clean and white, with a drip in his arm, staring at an improbably high ceiling. The shape that emerged from the fog turned out to be a doctor, who announced, without moving his lips, that cancer had taken up residence in Robert's right lung. He recommended a wedge resection. Robert refused. After a few days in hospital, he went home, with a stop at the dep for rolling papers and tobacco. His managers agreed to turn sick leave into early retirement. He continued his life's work, started revisiting his old haunts. Each day was a touch more painful than the last. He felt increasingly misunderstood. One night at Quai des Brumes, at a book launch for a young, good-looking poet whose name Robert didn't catch but whose reading was met with vociferous enthusiasm, he found the Poetry Van's summer schedule lying on a table.

8

We came back after New Year's, fat and flatulent from two weeks of too much food and alcohol. The running joke was to see how badly we could stink up the car, imprisoned in the cockpit through the requisite traffic jams on Highway 20. Even Jasmin and Chloé put aside the usual denials and claimed ownership of their poisonous emissions. Winter had been slow to reach the city. When we finally got moving, the snow was mixed with freezing rain. Passing cars sprayed us with a slushy mess. We took an early exit to an isolated gas station for windshield-washer fluid. I was trying to come home with the relatively good spirits I'd found in the Bois-Francs intact. The city soon reminded me of the harsh task awaiting me: I had to help my friend die.

On our first day back, a new copy-editing job came in. Jasmin went back to kindergarten, Chloé had daycare, Joannie wrote a few paragraphs of her dissertation. When the kids got home, I went to see Robert. Asleep, he breathed gently through his mouth despite the tubes in his nose. He'd taken a turn for the worse, but he was still himself. On the bedside table next to the phone lay the writing pad I'd brought him. I couldn't resist having a look. Every single page had something on it, a few words or some haphazard lines or the beginnings of a sketch. I gathered what consolation I could in the fact that he was still blackening pages, and I took the pad with me when I left. Out of respect for his work, I decided I'd deposit it in his archive the next day, on top of the most recent pile in his living room, and bring him a fresh one.

There are dozens of stories of artists who have lost their work. The Icelandic scholar Árni Magnússon watched parts of his priceless collection burn in the 1728 Copenhagen Fire. Whole Haydn symphonies went up in flames. Jolliet lost the journals of his Mississippi River expedition. There are countless other stories; history will never know the exact number. Not everything can be saved. There was no fire in Robert's apartment, but a story was unfolding there whose plot I didn't fully understand as I crossed Rue de Marseille and turned onto the sidewalk on Boulevard Langelier. Near the bottom of the hill, papers were flying around in the air, which had cooled, presaging a first snow. Closer to Robert's apartment, masses of paper and gutted notebooks were whirling around, tossed on the street by two thick dudes emptying out the apartment of the tenant who had disappeared. They made trip after trip with armfuls of documents, not even bothering to stack them next to the recycling bins lined up for collection. I went inside. Other men were tossing paper from the second-floor window into a dumpster in the yard, along with the debris from the bathroom they were demolishing with sledgehammers. They asked me no questions, just gave me a hard stare that made it clear I'd better leave. I spent a long time watching the flying papers and notebooks dancing around the first wet snowflakes. A woman stopped, intrigued by the pile, and picked up a notebook. She flipped through it, then laid it back down on the ground and walked away. When I saw her from behind, shrugging her shoulders, I was outraged. What I was witnessing was an affront to one man's memory, sure, but also, I feared, an affront to Literature, to the very possibility of Literature. I remembered how bad these texts had seemed to me, but still, confronted with this carnage, had to give them the benefit of the doubt. There just might be something there I hadn't understood or felt; my own poetry was mediocre at best, and I wasn't the most perspicacious reader. Of course, I could have missed something now disappearing into this winter day, onto the asphalt here in Mercier in the east end of Montreal, something that would be lost forever, something that had always carried a death sentence. No matter how weak or worthless, vain or incoherent, I thought, there was something of value in this life set down in writing. Somewhere in there was a voice that deserved to be heard. I picked up the notebook the woman had discarded and opened it. There was no epiphany. Just the same old spelling mistakes and platitudes I knew so well. And I at last saw the true nature of the oeuvre currently gliding to its final resting place, scattered over this shitty boulevard. It had always been about the writing itself. It had. But Robert had never arrived at any truth. All he'd ever done was borrow, imitate, slip through the cracks pretending, and pretending only to himself. It had been enough to keep him alive. It was awful. It was magnificent. I felt tears welling up. As I went up Langelier to the Metro, a recycling truck drove by. I hurled the notebook into its maw, along with the other one I'd brought from the hospital.

I went back to see Robert and sat down next to him. Time passed. I may have slept. When I decided it was time to go, he woke up and looked at me. 'Bastards took my notebook,' he whispered. I nodded. There was a dust bunny between my shoes. He touched me on the shoulder, pulled me toward him. 'I think it's the end. For real this time. Hard to believe. After living like that, nothing. Or just a bunch of bullshit. No, I don't believe it.' The dust didn't move. I breathed deeply. I put my hand in his and squeezed it, not too hard. And I answered. 'Don't worry, Robert. Go now. I'll try to figure something out for you.' And I left.

The author thanks Denise Brassard and Patrick Nicol for their illuminating readings of the the first version of this text. He also thanks the Conseil des arts et des lettres du Québec for financial assistance.

The translator thanks the author for his invaluable assistance, JC Sutcliffe for early feedback, Jeramy Dodds for translating the poem in Chapter 1, and Alana Wilcox for scrupulous editing.

Maxime Raymond Bock was born in the Rosemont neighbourhood of Montreal in 1981. He is currently pursuing a PhD. After various detours in sports and music, he published in 2011 a collection of stories, *Atavismes*, which won the Adrienne-Choquette Prize, and the novella *Rosemont en profil* in 2013. *Atavismes* was a first selection of the jury of the 2014 Jan Michalski Prize and was translated as *Atavisms* by Dalkey Archive Press in 2015.

Pablo Strauss grew up in British Columbia and now makes his home in Quebec City. He has translated short and long works by several Quebec authors, including Maxime Raymond Bock's *Atavisms*.

Typeset in Whitman.

Printed at the old Coach House on bpNichol Lane in Toronto, Ontario, on
Zephyr Antique Laid paper, which was manufactured, acid-free, in Saint-
Jérôme, Quebec, from second-growth forests. This book was printed with
vegetable-based ink on a 1965 Heidelberg KORD offset litho press. Its
pages were folded on a Baumfolder, gathered by hand, bound on a Sulby
Auto-Minabinda and trimmed on a Polar single-knife cutter.

Edited and designed by Alana Wilcox
Cover design by Ingrid Paulson

Coach House Books
80 bpNichol Lane
Toronto ON M5S 3J4
Canada

416 979 2217
800 367 6360

mail@chbooks.com
www.chbooks.com